The Egg Thieves

Joan Lingard was born in Edinburgh but grew up in Belfast. She has always been an avid reader and started writing when she was very young. She has now published more than thirty books for children.

She is married with three children and four grandchildren, and now lives in Edinburgh, Scotland.

Other Hodder story books you may enjoy:

TOM AND THE TREE HOUSE

WINNER OF THE SCOTTISH COUNCIL BOOK AWARD

Joan Lingard

THE FAIRY COW

Ann Turnbull

SECRET FRIENDS

Elizabeth Laird

THE DRAGON'S CHILD

Jenny Nimmo

FOG HOUNDS, WIND CAT, SEA MICE

Joan Aiken

The Egg Thieves

JOAN LINGARD

illustrated by Paul Howard

Hodder
Children's
Books

a division of Hodder Headline plc

Text copyright © 1999 by Joan Lingard
Illustrations copyright © 1999 by Paul Howard

First published in Great Britain in 1999
by Hodder Children's Books

10   9   8   7   6   5   4   3   2   1

A Catalogue record for this book is available from the British Library

ISBN 0340 73263 6

Printed and bound in Great Britain by
Richard Clay Ltd, Bungay, Suffolk

Hodder Children's Books
A Division of Hodder Headline plc
338 Euston Road

For Amy and Shona
with love

Chapter One

It was Lecky Grant who saw the egg thieves leaving. Something wakened him early that morning. He slipped out of bed and went to the window. His house was opposite the pine wood where the ospreys had their nest.

It was a misty morning. The trees had that shrouded, ghostly look that made you shiver a little. But the car that was sitting in the path that led into the wood had nothing to do with ghosts. It looked solid. And although the engine was running softly, Lecky could hear it clearly.

He ran through to his parents' bedroom shouting, 'Dad, egg thieves!'

He didn't wait for an answer but tore down the stairs in his bare feet and pyjamas. He yanked open the front door. The car was manoeuvring out on to the road.

'Stop!' Lecky dashed out in front of it waving his arms.

His father, coming up behind him, shouted, 'Get back, Lecky! Don't be an idiot!'

The car swerved round Lecky, its tyres screeching on the loose gravel at the side of the road. For a moment it looked as if it might mount the bank. Then it righted itself and, picking up speed, raced off.

'Never do that again!' said Mr Grant. 'You could have been killed.'

Now Mrs Grant appeared on the doorstep, pulling on her dressing gown. 'Come inside at once, Lecky!' she commanded. 'Look at you – out there in your pyjamas! *And* bare feet! You'll catch your death of cold. You, too,' she added to her husband.

They followed her into the kitchen. She filled the kettle while her husband phoned the police station. PC Murray said he'd be right along. He was the only policeman in the village.

'Bit late now, though, isn't it?' said Mrs Grant. 'Trying to lock the stable door when the horse has gone.'

'They might have left clues,' said Lecky hopefully. 'Footprints. Things like that. We should go and look, Dad.'

'Away and get yourself dressed first!' said his mother. 'I'm not wanting you going out into the wood half naked.'

Lecky dressed quickly. He had just finished when PC Murray arrived. The constable looked as if he hadn't had time to comb his hair.

Mrs Grant set a pot of tea on the table, and a pile of warm, buttered toast.

'Sit in,' she said. 'It's a chilly morning. Better to go out with something in your stomach.'

'It would have been egg thieves, I suppose?' said the constable, warming his hands round a mug of tea.

'Im afraid so,' said Mr Grant glumly. 'Who else would be parking there this early in the morning?'

'*And* they took off without lights,' said Lecky. 'So they must have been up to something.'

PC Murray sighed and brought out his notebook and ballpoint pen. 'Can you give me a description of the car?'

'Saloon,' said Mr Grant. 'Two door.'

'Don't suppose either of you got the car number?'

'There was mud over the number plate,' said Lecky.

'Aye, there would be! Camouflage. Colour?'

'Dark,' said Lecky.

The constable wrote that down. 'No

idea what colour of dark?'

'Navy blue. Maybe black. I'm not sure, are you, Dad? It all happened so quickly and it wasn't quite light.'

'That's when they come, these hooligans!' said the constable.

But they knew it was unlikely that they would have been hooligans out just to vandalise the nest. They'd have been proper egg thieves who would sell the eggs to collectors. Osprey eggs were rare and in demand. At one time the birds had been wiped out altogether in Britain.

'They'll be miles away by this time,' said Mr Grant. It was known that people would drive hundreds of miles to raid nests.

Some osprey nests were kept under constant watch by the Royal Society for the Protection of Birds. Their nest wasn't one of those. Lecky complained about that now.

'It's not fair!'

'The RSPB can't protect every single nest in the country,' said his father.

The local people tried to keep a watchful eye themselves on the ospreys. They thought of them as 'their' ospreys. The nest was meant to be a secret, but how could it be a real secret when everybody round about knew it was there?

'How many in the car?' asked PC Murray.

'Two,' said Lecky. 'Both in the front.'

'Male?'

'I think so.'

'Difficult to be absolutely certain,' said Mr Grant.

The constable nodded, closed his notebook and tucked it into his top pocket.

When they had drunk their tea and

eaten the toast, they crossed the road, Lecky, his dad, and PC Murray. They took a lightweight aluminium ladder with them and Mr Grant carried a long pole which had a mirror attached to its end.

On the track into the wood they saw the tyre marks the car had left in the mud. The thieves would have had no other choice but to park only a mere stone's throw from the road. Two large boulders blocked the rest of the path. They'd been put there to stop motorbikers getting into the wood. Or cars, carrying egg thieves!

'Look,' cried Lecky, 'footprints!'

They bent to examine them. They looked fresh.

'You can't tell anything from that lot,' said PC Murray. 'Just that they were wearing heavy boots.'

'One of them had spikes on their shoes, though,' Mr Grant pointed out.

PC Murray nodded. 'Good for climbing trees.'

The ospreys' nest was in a clearing, a little way into the wood, at the top of a very tall pine tree. Barbed wire encircled the lower part of the trunk. It was meant to deter thieves but it obviously hadn't.

The parent ospreys were not on the nest. They were sitting on the top of another tree close by, level with the nest, watching it closely. They were big birds,

roughly sixty centimetres in length, and their wing spans, at full stretch, would measure as much as one hundred and fifty centimetres. They were dark brown in colour, with white undersides.

'They've been, that's for sure!' said Mr Grant. 'The thieves. The female would be sitting on the nest if they hadn't.'

The nest was large – it would need to be to house such big birds. Perched right on the top of the tree, constructed mostly from large pieces of stick, it was a raggedy-looking affair. It could easily be seen from the ground below. Last year Lecky and his dad had found an abandoned nest. It had measured a metre across and seventy-five centimetres in depth.

Mr Grant took a closer look at the trunk of the tree just above the barbed wire. 'I can see the mark of his spikes.'

'Will you go up or will I?' asked PC Murray, who, it was well known, had a poor head for heights. Last year he'd had to rescue a kitten stuck halfway up a rowan tree. He'd felt dizzy before he'd got anywhere near her.

'I'll go,' said Mr Grant. He was a forester and didn't mind climbing tall trees. Neither did Lecky, but he knew his father wouldn't let him do it.

PC Murray propped the ladder against the trunk of the tree and Lecky helped him steady it. Mr Grant, with the pole held firmly in his hand, climbed slowly up. The ospreys didn't like this, not one little bit!

They uttered cries of alarm. They flapped their wings. They rose into the air, showing off their huge wing spans and white undersides. They looked magnificent and terrifying. They made you want to duck and cover your head with your arms. Lecky swallowed. What if they were to attack his dad?

'Sorry to do this to you, guys,' said Mr Grant, squinting up at them.

The birds continued to circle the treetops, flapping their wings and uttering fierce, threatening cries.

Mr Grant raised the long pole until the mirror was suspended over the nest and he could see inside. Lecky and PC Murray waited anxiously below.

'They've taken the lot!' said Mr Grant.

'Oh no!' cried Lecky.

'I'm afraid so,' said his dad. 'All three eggs are gone.'

Chapter Two

The whole village was furious, once the news spread. The talk that morning was of nothing else in the shop-cum-post office.

'The nerve of them!' said Nora McPhee, whose father was the postmaster. In the mornings, for half an hour before going to school, she helped her mother behind the shop counter. People came in at that time for milk and papers.

'It's no one from the village, anyway, that's obvious!' said Mrs McPhee.

'How can you tell that?' asked old Mr Taylor, who lived two doors away and had come along in his slippers to fetch his paper.

'Stands to reason, doesn't it? They were in a car. They must be outsiders.'

'Somebody local could have tipped them off.'

'You're right, Mr Taylor,' said Nora, finding that an interesting idea. 'They could!'

'Now who would do a thing like that?' said Mrs McPhee.

'I could think of someone,' said Mr Taylor knowingly.

They knew who he meant. Dod Smith, who lived up the back of the village in an old ramshackle cottage, had taken a brand new spade from Mr Taylor's shed last summer. Mr Taylor hadn't forgiven him even though he'd got it back. PC Murray had gone up to Dod's place and fetched it. Dod had said he'd only borrowed it, but he was known to be a bit 'light-fingered'. He never took anything much, usually a tool or something he needed. And often as not, when he'd finished with it, he'd return it.

'How would Dod know how to contact egg thieves?' demanded Mrs McPhee.

'He knows more than you think!' said Mr Taylor.

'I think that's enough on that subject,' put in Mr McPhee, who was sorting sheets of stamps at the post office counter.

The old man took his newspaper and shuffled out.

Mr McPhee shook his head. 'Too much gossip goes on in this place.'

'Mind you, I do remember seeing Dod talking to two men in a dark car back in the summer,' said Mrs McPhee. 'It wasn't a car I knew by sight.'

'Well, keep the information to yourself!' said her husband. 'You, too, Nora! They might just have been asking the way. We're not wanting to start false rumours.'

The school was also seething with the news of the theft. Lecky told his story several times over and Mrs Fraser, the teacher, asked him to write it up in the school diary.

Mrs Fraser was their only teacher. She lived in a house at the side of the school, along with her husband, who was the local vet, and their two children, Jessie and Johnny, aged six and seven. They were pupils at the school. There were seventeen pupils in all, ranging from

Primary One to Primary Seven. They worked in groups in the same room and the big ones helped the little ones. Their room was bright and cheerful and the walls were covered with stories and drawings and photographs. In pride of place was a large coloured photo of an osprey in flight, its wings stretched wide.

'Today,' wrote Lecky, 'a crime was committed in the wood.'

'A terrible crime,' insisted Nora, who was sitting beside him watching him write. 'Well, it was terrible. For the ospreys. And us.'

'Oh, all right.' He added, 'A terrible crime.'

'The criminals must be caught and punished,' said Nora. 'Put that down too!'

'I can put it down,' he scoffed. 'But who's going to catch them? Mr Murray says he's got nothing much to go on. There are too many dark cars on the roads.'

'I might have something to go on,' said Nora mysteriously.

'You!'

'I just could have an idea for a suspect,' she said, dropping her voice.

'Oh yes?' He knew Nora McPhee! She had a great imagination. 'So who do you think it is?'

'Tell you later.'

At breaktime, in the playground, they went over by the back wall. A ewe was feeding her lamb on the other side. The field was dotted with sheep. The noise of their bleating filled the air.

'Cross your heart, Lecky Grant, and promise you won't tell anyone else!' demanded Nora. 'My dad would kill me.'

'Tell them what?'

'Promise!'

'OK, I promise!' Lecky rolled his eyes. He was curious, though, to know who she had in mind. Some batty idea, more than likely.

'My mum saw Dod Smith talking to two men in a dark car last summer.'

'Is that all? *Hundreds* of dark cars come through the village every summer.'

'Not *hundreds*. Maybe one or two. But it wouldn't do any harm to check Dod out though, would it?'

'How do you think you can do that?'

Nora shrugged. 'We could take a walk up by his house when he's out.'

'And break in?'

'He never locks the door, you know that.' Most people in the village didn't, not in the daytime at least.

The bell rang to mark the end of break.

'What do you say?' asked Nora.

'I dunno,' said Lecky.

At lunchtime, Mrs Fraser took the children into the wood to look at the ospreys' nest. They stopped on the edge of the clearing.

'We must keep our distance,' said Mrs Fraser. 'We don't want to upset the birds even more.'

The two parent birds were still there, circling their empty nest. Round and round they went, aimlessly. They looked as if they didn't know what to do with themselves. The sight of them quietened the children.

'They must be hoping somebody will bring their eggs back,' said Nora.

'But they won't,' said Lecky gloomily.

'Poor birds,' said Mrs Fraser.

'They look awfully sad,' said Jessie, her daughter.

'You'd be sad if your babies got stolen,' said Nora.

'Won't they have any more?' asked Claire.

'Not this year,' said Lecky. 'And Dad

says they might not even come back to nest here next year.'

'I wish those thieves would come back here right now!' said Nora.

'We could trip them up,' said Rod Smith, sticking out his foot to show how he would do it.

'And tie them up!' said Tommy Rankin, lassooing them with an imaginary rope.

'And drag them along to the police station!' said Nora.

'That'd be right!' said Lecky. 'I could just see you!'

'We've got to do something about these egg thieves,' said Nora.

'There's not much we can do this year. It's too late.'

'We could start a protection society of our own.'

'Hey, that's a good idea!' said Tommy.

'Yes, I think it would be a good idea,' said Mrs Fraser.

They turned as they heard heavy feet crackling on fallen branches. Two men were coming their way. But it wasn't the egg thieves returning to the scene of their crime. It was a reporter from the local paper and a photographer with a heavy camera hanging round his neck.

The photographer had come to photograph the tree and the nest and the two unhappy parent birds. He took quite a while doing it, taking them from this angle and that. He even lay on his back on the ground.

The reporter interviewed Lecky. It must have been the tenth time he'd told his story!

'So how do you kids feel about this?' asked the reporter, his pen poised above his pad. 'Can you give me a quote?'

'We're furious!' said Nora.

The reporter wrote that down.

'It's like getting your house burgled,' said Claire. Her auntie's house in Glasgow had been burgled a week or two back. Her auntie hadn't had a wink of sleep since.

'We're planning to set up our own osprey protection society,' said Nora.

The reporter was scribbling away.

'We're going to stop them doing this again!' vowed Lecky.

'They'll not get away with it another time!' cried Nora.

On the way back to school, she said to Lecky, 'What about Dod Smith?'

'What about him? You've only got old Mr Taylor's gossip to go on.'

'I suppose you're right,' sighed Nora.

They forgot all about Dod Smith, in the meantime.

Chapter Three

ANGRY CHILDREN SET UP
OSPREY WATCH!

So ran the headline in the paper when it came out the following Thursday. The paper was published only once a week.

Mrs Fraser read the article aloud to them: 'Local children are so angry that the ospreys' eggs have been stolen that they have vowed to set up a protection society. They said they were determined to stop the egg thieves from stealing the eggs next year.'

She pinned the cutting on the noticeboard and the children wrote stories and poems about the ospreys. The first and second year infants drew pictures of a man pulling eggs from the nest. The men in their drawings had enormous heads, bulging eyes and long, snaky fingers. All the work was put up on the wall.

After a while the pictures and stories came down to make way for new ones, but the newspaper cutting stayed on the board throughout the summer and the following winter. It was looking a bit yellow and frayed at the edges by the time March blew in wild and windy. Snow fell on the hills but melted quickly down in the village. The ospreys usually came back at the beginning of April.

The children began to talk again about their protection society.

'We ought to build a hide,' said Lecky.

The older children went into the wood after school. When they arrived at the clearing they saw that the ospreys' nest had been damaged by the winter storms. Part of one side was hanging out.

'They won't want to come back to that, will they?' said Nora.

'If they do come back they'll mend it,' said Lecky.

Mr Grant helped them choose a spot for the hide, well back from the nest. He picked a slightly raised mound some thirty metres away. When he stood on top of it he could see the nest through his binoculars.

'Yes, this would be a good spot.'

The wood here was ramshackle.

Several old trees had had their trunks split in the high winds. Others had been completely blown down. Branches lay higgledy-piggledy over the ground, making it difficult to pick a way through.

They set to work. They cleared a space, then using fallen branches and some strong sacking material they made a tent-like structure in the shelter of two or three young, low trees.

'It looks a bit like one of those Indian tepees,' said Tommy.

The hide would hold two comfortably, three at a pinch.

'We'll take it in turns to watch,' said Lecky.

'We could draw up a rota,' suggested Tommy.

'A good idea,' said Nora.

'We can't be here *all* the time though, can we?' said Claire. 'My mum wouldn't let me come in the morning while it's still dark.'

'My dad will be keeping a look-out as well,' said Lecky.

'So will mine,' said Calum Murray, whose father was the police constable.

'That didn't stop them before, did it?' said Nora.

'But this year *everybody* will be watching for thieves!' said Lecky.

April came in, still windy and wet, but the daffodils were out and a few purple and yellow crocuses peeked through the hard ground. The first lambs were born and starting to stagger about on wobbly legs in the field at the back of the school wall.

The children waited anxiously for any sign of the ospreys. The first day of the first week passed. And the second day. And the third.

'They may not come back,' Mr Grant reminded them. 'You have to be prepared for that.'

Lecky rose early every morning and sat at his window with his binoculars. He kept them trained on the wood.

On the fifth day he made a sighting.

'Dad,' he yelled, running into his parents' room, 'the ospreys are back!'

He knew it would be the male bird.

He always came back first to check on the nest or to begin building a new one.

Lecky didn't say anything in class that day as he didn't want everyone to go barging into the wood to disturb the osprey.

'What are you up to today?' asked Nora.

'Nothing.' He tried to look innocent.

'You keep smiling to yourself,' she said suspiciously.

'What's wrong with smiling?' he asked.

He hurried home after school, giving Nora the slip. His father was waiting for him. They took their binoculars and went cautiously into the wood, taking care to make as little noise as possible. They slipped into the hide.

The osprey was flying in wide circles high above his old nest, clearly visible against the blue and white of the sky. He was displaying the full span of his wings. He looked magnificent, flying away up there above the treetops.

'He's showing off,' said Mr Grant softly. 'He must be nearly three hundred metres up! He's telling the world – stay away from my space!'

Someone was coming. Someone with coppery red hair. It was Nora! Who else? Lecky groaned. She was trying to walk on tiptoe but her feet were making the fallen branches crackle and snap.

'Be quiet!' he whispered.

'No need to shout!'

He glared at her but he moved over to make room. His dad let her look through his binoculars. She'd just got them between her hands when the osprey flew off.

'He's gone!' she cried. And Lecky would probably blame her for chasing him away!

'He'll be back, I expect,' said Mr Grant. 'He may have gone for nesting material.'

'That would mean he intends to stay!' said Lecky excitedly.

They waited patiently and ten minutes later the osprey returned with a long stick clenched firmly in his talons. It looked like a piece of dead branch.

He began to fly in wide circles again, as he had done before, high above his eyrie. Then, suddenly, he climbed even higher, making fast wing beats. He gave a high-pitched call. He hovered. Now he was diving rapidly down. He landed on the nest.

The three watchers sighed with relief. The bird's head twitched. He was listening and watching. The stick he was holding must

have been nearly a metre long. After a few minutes he seemed to decide it was safe to start work. He began by pitching out the old lining. Mr Grant raised his thumb in triumph and Lecky and Nora grinned at each other. They stayed for an hour in the hide and then went back to the village to spread the good news.

The following day, the female osprey returned. She was even bigger than the male. Both birds would have spent the winter in West Africa.

'But not together,' said Mr Grant.

'Gosh!' Nora found that amazing. 'Do you mean they haven't seen one another since the end of last summer?'

'That's right.'

And yet they had found each other, just like that.

'*And* their nest,' said Mr Grant.

'They're so clever,' said Nora. Imagine

finding the way back from Africa to this particular wood, to this particular tree! She and Lecky had almost got lost in the wood once and they'd known it ever since they could walk.

The birds were busy, intent on the task in hand. They were rebuilding their home. They flew to and fro, to and fro, carrying bits of bark, moss and turf for the lining of the nest. From time to time the male bird went off to fish. Lecky's dad told them that ospreys would travel to lochs and rivers up to ten miles away. When the bird brought a fish back his mate joined him in a nearby tree for the feast. They never ate in the nest.

'I'm going to call them Oona and Ollie,' said Nora. The names caught on.

At school that week, all the drawings on the wall were of ospreys: ospreys in full flight with wings expanded; ospreys repairing their nest; ospreys diving for fish in the river.

'I think you should stay away from the wood until the nest is built and the female has laid her eggs,' said Mrs Fraser.

At the end of the month Lecky and his dad saw the female osprey sitting on the nest.

'It seems Oona's laid an egg!' said Lecky, when he came into school that morning. 'She'll not budge much now. And when she does Ollie will keep guard.'

The children were excited. They drew nests with one large egg sitting in the centre. Osprey eggs were white with chocolate-coloured splotches and, surprisingly, no larger than hens' eggs.

In the next few days Mr Grant thought

the female might have laid two more eggs. He decided to go up the tree to look. He took the long pole again, with the mirror on the end of it. While he was up the tree Oona flew off and squawked and flapped around but she settled down quickly again afterwards.

'There are three eggs there,' Mr Grant confirmed.

Lecky brought the news to school again and recorded it in the diary. 'It'll take thirty-five to forty days for them to hatch.'

'That's an awful lot of days to wait,' groaned Claire. 'More than a month.'

'And it's an awful lot of days for the egg thieves to strike!' said Nora.

'Yes,' agreed Lecky, 'now is the dangerous time. We must start our watch.'

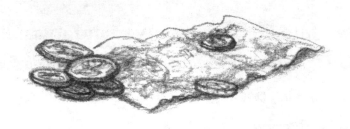

Chapter Four

'**D**od Smith seems to be in the money these days,' commented Mrs McPhee.

'What did you say?' demanded Nora, pricking up her ears.

It was Saturday morning and she was in the shop giving her mother a hand. She liked being in the shop and having the chance to chat to people as they came in and out. There was usually a bit of bustle on Saturdays.

'Usually he hasn't two pennies to rub together.' Mrs McPhee then broke off to say, 'Don't just sit there reading those comics, Nora! Get them out on the shelf. And I'm not wanting them all creased before you do.'

'So usually Dod doesn't have two pennies to rub together,' she reminded her mother.

'It's just that he seems to be spending a lot these days,' said Mrs McPhee, with an eye on her husband who was at the back of the post office counter. 'He bought a new TV last week. The delivery man called here to ask the way to his house.'

At that point the door opened and in came Dod himself.

'Dod!' exclaimed Nora in surprise.

Her mother gave her a look which said, 'Don't be saying anything about his TV!'

'How are you doing, Nora?' asked Dod.

'Fine,' she replied, eyeing his sweater which she could see beneath his open anorak. It was bright scarlet, which matched his woollen hat, and it looked brand new. The hat wasn't new. It had seen many a winter. Dod and new clothes didn't seem to go together. Nora had only ever seen him in a shabby old khaki-coloured jersey, scruffy trousers and tackity boots. 'I like your sweater,' she said.

'Do you?' He was pleased. 'I got it in the town last Saturday.'

'Are you going to town today?'

'I am indeed. I'm getting the eleven bus.'

It was ten to now.

'I've come in for some mints. I like a sweetie to suck on the bus.'

Nora served him.

'Have you any shopping to get in the town today?' she asked casually. At least she was trying to sound casual.

'I might get myself a pair of trousers. You know those kind with all the pockets down the legs?'

'They'd be handy right enough,' put in Mrs McPhee.

'That's what I think. I could keep all my bits and pieces in them.'

Dod took his mints and went out to wait for the bus.

'He does seem to be in the money, doesn't he?' said Nora.

The bus came along in the next few minutes. She watched through the window as Dod clambered aboard, the pom-pom on top of his hat bobbing busily.

'Do you need me now?' she asked, sliding out from behind the counter.

'I suppose you're wanting away,' said her mother.

Nora pulled on her anorak. 'Won't be long.'

The street was empty, now that the bus had gone. She walked quickly, passing old Mr Taylor's long, low cottage without a sideways glance, then the pub, then Claire's house, which was set back a bit from the road, and then the church and the manse. The minister was standing at his door. She gave him a wave but didn't stop. She didn't want to waste any time. When she reached the end of the street she broke into a run.

Lecky lived half a mile down the road. He was at home.

'He's upstairs working on his aeroplane model,' said his mother, who was baking scones. The smell made Nora's mouth water. Lecky's mother was the best baker in the village. She always took first prize at the cake baking competitions at the fête. Nora's own mum didn't have time to bake, with being in the shop all day.

Lecky was absorbed in his aeroplane kit. 'Hang on a minute,' he cried. 'I'm at a tricky part.'

Nora moved from one foot to the other as he glued the part into place.

'OK,' he said finally.

'You remember I told you Mr Taylor thought Dod Smith might be the one who leaked the ospreys' nest to the egg thieves?'

'Not that again!'

'No, wait, Lecky!' Nora told him about Dod coming in to money. 'So don't you think we should go and check him out?'

'And what do you think we would find?'

'I dunno. But maybe something.'

'You're off the wall, Nora McPhee.'

'I am not, Lecky Grant! Well, I'm going up to his house.' Nora tossed her head. 'You needn't come if you don't want to.'

'I guess I'd better. To see you don't do anything stupid!'

She knew he'd come. He'd be too curious not to.

Mrs Grant gave them a hot scone dripping with butter and they left, saying they were going for a walk. They took the road that went up behind the village.

On the way they met PC Murray in his car. He stopped and put his head out of the window.

'What are you two up to this morning?' he asked.

'Nothing,' said Nora.

'Bird watching, I'll bet, if I know Lecky!'

He didn't wait for an answer but went rolling on down the hill. There was no one else about and no noise but for the sound of the wind and the calling of the sheep. Dod's cottage stood alone, well away from any other.

They slid over the dyke and crossed the stretch of moorland that led to it, dodging the sheep. Dod kept only a few, as well as a couple of goats and some chickens which were pecking at the ground close to the house.

'It's against the law, you know,' said Lecky, 'breaking into someone else's house.'

'We won't have to *break* in,' said Nora. 'Not if the door's open.'

It wasn't.

'That's funny.' Nora frowned. 'He doesn't usually lock the door, I know he doesn't. My dad brings shopping up for him and he just opens the door and puts it in.'

'Maybe he felt like locking it today.'

'Maybe he had something to hide! I wonder where he's left the key.'

Nora looked under a boulder lying close by. It wasn't there. Lecky kicked aside a few other stones.

'Probably took it with him,' he said.

'It must be a big key. To fit that lock ...'

Nora went round the side. She bent down. 'Got it!' she cried. The key was tucked behind the pipe where it came down to the drain.

'We're still not having to *break* in,' she said, fitting the key in the lock.

'But it's trespassing.'

'You chicken?'

'You joking?' Lecky went in ahead of her.

It was dark inside the house. Something leapt out of a doorway and Nora jumped and screamed.

'It's only a cat, stupid!' said Lecky.

They went into the living room-cum-kitchen. The place was in a terrible mess. Dirty dishes and pots littered the draining board and table. The floor was covered with old newspapers, socks, boots and cat dishes. The furniture was ancient and tatty.

'What a pong!' Nora wrinkled her nose.

'He never opens the windows,' said Lecky.

Nora began to hunt vaguely around.

'What is it that you think you're looking for?' asked Lecky.

'Evidence.'

'Evidence!' He snorted. 'All this tells us is that Dod's no good at housework.' He kept watch at the window in case someone might be coming. At the moment all he could see were sheep grazing on the bits of grass in between the heather.

Suddenly he straightened up. 'Hey, Nora, it's the postie!'

They hadn't reckoned on Dod getting mail. The red post van was coming bumping up the rough track towards the house.

'We'll have to hide,' said Nora.

Lecky opened a door. It led into the coal cellar though there were only a few bits of coal in it. Dod would mostly burn logs which he stored outside. The cupboard smelt strongly of coal. They had no choice. The postie was slamming the door of his van. They crammed themselves into the cupboard and pulled the door shut. It was pitch black inside and there was no air.

'Can't breathe,' said Nora.

'Too bad,' said Lecky.

The front door was opening.

'Dod?' called the postie. 'Are you there, Doddie? I've got a parcel for you.'

They heard the postie's feet coming along the passage and into the room. He must be standing only a metre or two from them!

Nora thought she would explode. The smell of the coal dust was making her feel sick and her nose was prickling like mad. She could feel a huge sneeze building up. She pinched her nostrils tightly between her fingers. If she didn't get out of here soon she would throw up, or faint.

Then the footsteps moved away. The front door closed. Lecky opened the cupboard door a crack letting in light and air. They listened. They heard the sound of an engine.

'He's going,' said Lecky.

They emerged from the coal cellar. Nora let out an enormous sneeze. Then she began to laugh.

'Look at you, Lecky Grant, you're all sooty!'

'Look at yourself, Nora McPhee! Talk about the pot calling the kettle black!'

'The postie left Dod's parcel,' said Nora.

It was a bulky package.

'Don't touch it!' warned Lecky as she went to lift it. 'You'll make it dirty.'

'Looks like something ordered out of a catalogue,' said Nora. 'It is amazing that Dod can suddenly buy so much stuff.'

'Come on, let's go!' said Lecky. 'Before anyone else comes.'

'But we haven't had a proper look round.'

'There's nothing to see.'

Nora peeked under a cushion on the seat of an armchair.

'What's this?' she cried.

She wiped her hands on her jeans and pulled out an envelope. It crackled. It wasn't sealed. She lifted the flap. They looked inside.

'Money,' said Lecky in a whisper.

'A lot of money.'

They counted it. It came to two hundred pounds. Where *would* Dod get two hundred pounds?

Chapter Five

They puzzled over Dod's two hundred pounds all week but there was no way that they could find out how he'd got it. Even Nora didn't have enough cheek to ask him. He was going about the village in his new trousers, showing everyone all the different pockets he had. Nora admired them.

'They're great, aren't they?' He grinned. He had a spanner in one pocket and some rusty nails in another.

'Are you going shopping this

Saturday?' she asked.

'I'm not sure that I'll be needing anything.'

On Saturday morning, Nora was again in the shop. Dod didn't come in. The eleven o'clock bus came and went.

A little while later, a strange car pulled up in front of the post office. Nora craned her neck to see. A man and a woman were getting out. She'd never seen them before. They glanced around the street for a moment or two then they came into the shop.

'We believe there's an osprey nest in the area?' said the woman in a chatty voice.

'Couldn't tell you,' said Mrs McPhee, who was sorting a box of chocolate bars. She didn't look up.

The man leaned on the counter. 'You must have some idea where it is?'

'We're very keen bird watchers, you see.' The woman gave a big smile that was wasted on Mrs McPhee.

'Sorry I can't help you,' she said.

Nora kept her eye on them. They often did have people coming in to ask about the ospreys and they never let on to them that they knew where the nest was. But she didn't think they'd be so open about it if they *were* thieves. You never knew, though, did you?

The couple left. Nora watched them as they got back into their car and drove off. She snaffled a chocolate bar and drifted up the street after them. They'd gone only a little way down the road and parked in a lay-by beside the wood.

They hailed her. 'Hello, there, dear!' said the woman.

'We're really keen to find the ospreys,' said the man.

'You wouldn't know where they are, would you?' asked the woman.

'I think it's over that way.' Nora pointed across the road, on the opposite side from the nest.

The man turned to the woman. 'What do you think?'

'Might as well give it a go.'

'Thanks,' said the man to Nora.

They disappeared into the wood, taking the direction she had suggested. She smiled. She heard the couple crashing about between the trees. They certainly weren't true bird watchers, not if they went stumbling about like that. They'd scare anything off for miles.

She called at Lecky's house and his mother said he'd gone into the wood. 'He's been in there most of the day!'

Nora remembered that she was supposed to be in the hide with him that morning! It was on the rota. They'd been keeping watch after school every day, but there'd been nothing out of the way to report. The female was sitting on the nest and the male was bringing back food.

Nora found Lecky in the hide. She got in beside him and told him about the man and woman.

'They're probably just curious,' said Lecky.

Nora nodded. She broke her chocolate bar in two and passed half to him. They munched quietly and took turns to watch through the binoculars. Oona was on the nest. There was no sign of Ollie.

'He's probably gone fishing,' said Lecky.

Oona seemed a bit disturbed.

'What's up with her?' asked Nora.

'Don't know.' Lecky frowned.

Oona was moving around. She appeared to be pecking at something.

'It's an egg!' said Lecky.

'She's not eating it, is she?'

'I think it must be damaged. She's testing it to find out.'

Oona pecked for another minute or two, then she took the egg into her beak and flew to a neighbouring tree.

'What's she going to do?' cried Nora.

Oona looked down at the ground, opened her beak and dropped the egg.

'Oh no!' cried Nora.

'It must have been cracked,' said Lecky sadly.

Oona flew back to the nest and squatted on the remaining eggs.

'Now there are only two' said Nora.

'Let's hope no more get damaged!' said Lecky.

'Or stolen,' said Nora. 'It's not easy for them, is it? Having babies?'

They were about to go home for lunch when they heard someone coming. It didn't sound like the couple who'd been in the car. This person was treading carefully, trying not to make a noise.

They saw a movement through the branches. They thought it might be a man wearing a dark green jacket. A lot of people wore green jackets, especially in the country. He wasn't close enough for them to make him out properly. He was heading in the direction of the ospreys' nest. Now he was stopping. He was making no noise at all. Lecky and Nora made none either.

They stayed like that for a few minutes, afraid almost to breathe, then they heard him again. He was coming back. This time he passed closer to the hide.

When he came into their sight-line they saw that the man was Dod Smith and that he had a pair of binoculars round his neck.

They crept out of the hide and followed him out of the wood and up the road, keeping a good distance between them. Dod stopped in the village and went into the phone box.

'He's phoning someone!' said Nora excitedly.

'Could be anybody,' said Lecky.

'Could be an egg thief!'

They hovered around until he'd finished his call. When he came out of the box Nora called over to him.

'Hi, Dod!'

'Oh, hello, didn't see you there!'

'Are those new binoculars that you've got?' she asked Nora.

'I just got them yesterday. From one of those catalogue things. Through the mail, you know. Want to see?'

He unstrapped the case and took out the glasses. He allowed each of them to look through the lenses in turn.

'They're really good ones!' said Lecky.

'We saw you in the wood, Dod,' said Nora.

'I was just trying the binoculars out. Taking a wee look at the birds.'

'At the ospreys?' said Nora.

'Aye, the ospreys. Great looking birds.'

Dod put the binoculars back in their case and set off up the hill whistling.

'He must have come into a fortune,' said Lecky.

'Or else someone's paying him for information,' said Nora.

chapter six

They were all quite jumpy now about the eggs. There were still a lot of days to go before they would hatch out. The nights were moonlit, a good time for thieves to strike. Lecky found it difficult to get to sleep at nights. Every time he heard a noise he jumped up and went to the window. Every time a strange car came through the village the children stared after it as if it might contain the thieves. If they could they noted down the registration number. Nora kept a notebook on the shop counter to record the numbers.

Lecky's dad rose early each morning to go into the wood and check the nest.

'So far, so good,' he'd report at breakfast-time.

On Sunday evening, Mr Grant had to go and visit his mother. She'd rung to say she wasn't feeling well and could he come over. She lived thirty miles away.

'Want to come with me, Lecky?' he asked.

'I said I'd play table tennis.'

Mr Grant told his wife that he shouldn't be too late back.

Lecky went along to Nora's house, which was attached to the post office. She had a table tennis table set up in her garage. Her mum and dad kept their car in the street, except in mid-winter when it snowed or the frosts were severe.

Calum and Claire arrived soon after Lecky to make up a foursome. They left the door of the garage open on to the street for air. They played a few games and then took a break.

While they were drinking the Coke that Nora's mother had handed in, they saw a car sweep past. Not many cars came through the village on a Sunday evening.

'Strangers,' said Nora, going out into the street to gaze after it. 'Dark car.'

'Too early in the evening for egg thieves,' said Lecky.

'They might think they'd fool us by coming early,' said Nora. 'I mean, you wouldn't *expect* them at this time, would you?'

'She's right,' said Calum. 'And it *is* just beginning to get dark.'

'I think we should check them out.'
Nora put down her Coke tin. 'Make sure
they've gone.'

Claire had to go home. Her granny
was visiting for the night and
would want to see her. The others
accompanied Claire as far as her house,
then went on through the village. The
street was dead. Not even a cat was on
the move. Most people would be inside
watching television.

They carried on down the road, past
the church and the manse. When they
turned the first corner they couldn't see
any sign of the car.

'They could have parked round the
next bend,' said Nora.

'They could have parked ten miles
away!' said Lecky.

They walked on, anyway.

Suddenly Lecky shouted, 'Get down!'

They flattened themselves on the ground.

Up ahead, two men in dark clothes had rounded the bend and were coming towards them. They were keeping close to the trees, skirting the edge of the wood.

Lecky raised his head a little to get a better look. 'I don't think they saw us. They're making for the path into the wood!'

'That will take them straight to the nest!' said Nora.

'They're going into the wood now!' Lecky jumped up.

'Looks like they could be our egg thieves!' cried Nora.

'We've got to stop them before they get to the eggs!' said Lecky. 'You'd better go for your dad, Calum. Pity mine's away!' The Grants' house was closer.

'Tell your dad two men are acting suspiciously in the wood, Calum,' urged Nora.

'Tell him to come quickly,' added Lecky. 'And to bring someone else with him if he can!' There were *two* men, after all.

Calum sprinted off.

'We'll cut into the wood from here,' said Lecky. 'They might have a look-out on the track.' He led the way in through the trees, pushing aside overhanging branches. Nora followed.

'No talking, now!' he warned.

'You don't have to tell me, Lecky Grant!'

The route they were taking was more difficult than their usual one. There was no definite path to follow. They had to climb over felled trees and scramble under fallen branches. But Lecky knew the wood well. He could have found his way blindfold.

They stopped for a moment to listen. The faint rustling noises they could hear might be made by men or animals. Deer roamed freely in the wood.

Lecky nodded to Nora and they moved on. He was aiming to come in to the right of the ospreys' tree. Every few steps he paused to glance up, to check whether the nest was in sight. The moon was out now, lighting up the treetops.

He drew in a sharp breath and stopped so abruptly that Nora almost tripped on his heels. He grabbed her arm to quieten her and pointed at the sky. Looking up, she saw what he had seen. Ollie was in flight, high overhead, veering in wide circles, flapping his wings and giving forth frantic cries.

'Maybe we're too late!' cried Nora.

'Come on!' yelled Lecky and he went crashing off through the undergrowth. Nora dashed after him.

They reached the clearing in time to see a man in the process of climbing the osprey tree. They saw him clearly in the white moonlight. He was dressed in black from head to foot. A balaclava covered his head. He was about ten feet from the ground, just above the barbed wire.

Chapter Seven

'Get off!' screamed Lecky. 'Leave that nest alone!'

The man looked down, startled. They'd taken him by surprise. He stayed motionless for a few seconds leaning his body in against the trunk of the tree, as if he were uncertain as to what to do next. Ollie was continuing to squawk loudly overhead, with Oona joining in from the nest. She hadn't yet abandoned it.

'Get down!' cried Lecky again.

The noise had alerted the other man, who must have been on the look-out further down the path. He came running. The one on the tree began to climb again.

'Oh, no!' groaned Nora. 'Hang in there, Oona!'

The look-out was also dressed in black and wearing a balaclava. They couldn't see his face, only his eyes glittering in the slit. That was the most terrifying part of him. They were so frightened that they felt stuck to the ground. He stood in front of them, towering above them.

'Get out of here, you kids!' he commanded. 'Fast! If you know what's good for you!'

'The police are coming,' said Lecky.

'Don't give me that!'

At that moment they heard shouts and

the sound of feet drumming on the path.

'They're coming!' cried Nora. 'They are!'

The man on the ground spun round. He hesitated but only for a second before deciding to make a run for it. He went headlong into the trees.

They turned to see what the man up the tree would do. He was holding on to the trunk still but leaning out from it. Now he jumped! He came flying down through the air like a great heavy black bird. The children stood back.

As he was picking himself up Nora put out her foot and tripped him. He went sprawling face down on the ground. She raised her arms above her head and cheered.

By now PC Murray had arrived, panting, in the clearing, followed by Calum and four other men from the

village whom he'd collected on the way. Both Nora's and Lecky's fathers were amongst them. Mr Grant had just returned from visiting his mother.

'So this is one of them, I presume,' said PC Murray, hauling the man to his feet and clipping on handcuffs.

'It is,' said Lecky.

'He was up the tree,' said Nora.

PC Murray pulled the balaclava down off the man's face. No one there had ever seen him before.

'The other man ran off,' said Nora. 'He went that way. Into the wood.'

'He'll not find his way out of there very easily,' said Mr Grant. 'That part's a bit of a jungle.'

'We think they might have parked their car further on down the road,' said Lecky. 'Round the bend. He might try to make for that.'

'Right, lads!' said PC Murray. 'Let's go and find it!'

They found the car before the runaway did. It was the car the children had seen earlier. The thieves had left it on the edge of the wood, just off the road.

'He must still be wandering about in the wood,' said Lecky.

'Serve him right!' said Nora. 'Horrible man!'

The handcuffed man was saying nothing. He was keeping his head down and his eyes on the ground.

'You should be away home to your bed, Nora,' said her father.

But she didn't go and he didn't make her. Other people from the village had come out now and were gathered in the road. News always travelled fast.

It was almost an hour later before the

second thief emerged from the wood. He looked bedraggled. Bits of branch and bark clung to his balaclava. He seemed astounded to see such a crowd awaiting him. He was about to turn and run again when he thought better of it. After all, where could he go?

'Come quietly, sir,' said PC Murray. 'I'm arresting you both for attempting to steal eggs from the osprey nest in this wood.'

The man came quietly and took off his balaclava when instructed. He, too, stared at the ground.

Mr Grant was eyeing him and frowning. 'Hey, I know you, don't I?' The man looked up. 'You drive a truck for one of the forestry's timber contractors! So that's how you know about our nest!'

Nora and Lecky looked at each other. They were both thinking the same thing. They'd been wrong about Dod!

PC Murray was radioing for help to the police station in the town. He couldn't cope on his own with two arrests. A couple of constables came in a squad car and took the men away. The villagers made their way home. PC Murray said the men would get probably get very heavy fines. 'The last ones to be caught were fined a few thousand.'

In the morning, at first light, Lecky and his father went back into the woods to see how the ospreys were faring after their adventure. Oona was sitting on the nest and Ollie was keeping close watch.

'They should be all right now,' said Mr Grant. 'Though we'll still need to keep an eye open in case there are any other thieves about.'

In school they wrote stories and drew pictures of PC Murray arresting the egg thieves. The little children drew enormous pairs of handcuffs.

At lunchtime, Nora went home and returned with a round tin.

'What's in there?' asked Lecky.

'A chocolate cake. I made it yesterday. It's got hundreds and thousands and chocolate buttons on top. I'm going to give it to Dod. I feel awful about suspecting him. And he was innocent all the time!'

'I suspected him too, didn't I?'

'But it was me that started it,' she said miserably.

Lecky went with her after school. Dod was pottering about outside his door.

'Dod,' said Nora, presenting him with the tin, 'this is for you.'

'For me?' He lifted the lid and looked inside. 'A *cake?* You're giving it to *me?*'

Nora nodded.

'Nobody's ever given me a cake before. How did you know it was my birthday? You must have second sight!'

Nora did not deny it. She avoided

Lecky's eye. For of course she hadn't known it was Dod's birthday.

'Come on in,' he said. 'And I'll make you a wee cup of tea.'

They had seen the state of his kitchen so they weren't too keen on the idea of a cup of tea. But they went in anyway.

Dod's tea tasted like tar. They sipped it slowly from thick, cracked mugs. He put the cake on a plate and cut it with a knife that he kept for gutting fish. They each had a slice.

'That's fantastic cake, Nora!' said Dod. 'The best I've ever eaten. How do you like my new teapot?' He held it up for them to admire. It was blue, and decorated with red roses. 'Pretty, eh?'

Lecky nodded. His mouth was too full of sticky chocolate sponge to speak. The cake wasn't bad though, considering Nora had made it.

'You've been treating yourself quite a bit lately, Dod,' said Nora.

He chuckled. 'I have that. Will I let you into a secret?'

'Please!'

'I had a win on the lottery last year! Not a big win, you understand, but big enough for me. A few thousand.'

'A few thousand!' echoed Nora. She would call that big.

'Wow!' said Lecky.

'You did manage to keep it secret, didn't you?' said Nora.

'You'll not be telling, will you? I'm not wanting the whole village to know. They'd be up here trying to borrow money from me.'

'Don't worry, Dod,' said Nora, 'I promise you I'll never ever tell! Cross my heart!'

'And you'd better not tell anyone!' said Lecky when they were going back down the hill afterwards.

'I won't!' said Nora indignantly. 'Of course I won't! Dod's our friend now, isn't he?'

Two weeks later, two osprey chicks were safely hatched. Their birth was recorded in the school diary. Everyone in the village was delighted. The talk in the shop was of nothing else.

Lecky and Nora went up to Dod's house after school and asked him if he'd like to come down to their hide to look at the ospreys.

'Thanks very much,' he said. 'I'd like that fine.'

He fetched his new binoculars. Lecky had brought his with him and Nora had borrowed her father's.

They crept quietly into the hide. There was just room for the three of them, with a bit of a squash. They trained their binoculars on the hide.

Oona was on the nest.

'Do you see the babies' beaks sticking up?' asked Lecky.

'Aye,' nodded Dod, 'I do.'

'Oh, look!' whispered Nora excitedly. 'Oona's just popped a bit of fish into one of the beaks! Gobble, gobble, it's gone!'

'That's a great sight!' said Dod.

'It is, isn't it?' said Lecky happily.

'They're safe from those horrible men now,' said Nora with a sigh.

'You should get a medal,' declared Dod. 'You should! The two of you. For catching the egg thieves.'